North of Hope

JON HASSLER

Introduction by Amy Welborn

LOYOLA CLASSICS

CHICAGO

LOYOLAPRESS.

3441 N. ASHLAND AVENUE
CHICAGO, ILLINOIS 60657
(800) 621-1008
WWW.LOYOLAPRESS.ORG

Previously published in the United States by Ballantine Books, a division of Random House, Inc., New York, and simultaneously in Canada by Random House of Canada Limited, Toronto.

Series art direction: Adam Moroschan
Series design: Adam Moroschan and Erin VanWerden
Cover design: Erin VanWerden
Interior design: Erin VanWerden

Library of Congress Cataloging-in-Publication Data
Hassleer, Jon.
  North of hope / Jon Hassler.
    p. cm.—(Loyola classics series)
  ISBN 0-8294-2357-5
  1. Catholics—Fiction. 2. Clergy—Fiction. I. Title. II. Series.
PS3558.A726N67 2006
813'.54—dc22

                                        2005029708

Printed in the United States of America
06 07 08 09 10 Bang 10 9 8 7 6 5 4 3 2 1